Books by Paige Sleuth

Cozy Cat Caper Mystery Series:
Murder in Cherry Hills (Book 1)
Framed in Cherry Hills (Book 2)
Poisoned in Cherry Hills (Book 3)
Vanished in Cherry Hills (Book 4)
Shot in Cherry Hills (Book 5)
Strangled in Cherry Hills (Book 6)
Halloween in Cherry Hills (Book 7)
Stabbed in Cherry Hills (Book 8)
Thanksgiving in Cherry Hills (Book 9)
Frozen in Cherry Hills (Book 10)
Hit & Run in Cherry Hills (Book 11)
Christmas in Cherry Hills (Book 12)
Choked in Cherry Hills (Book 13)
Dropped Dead in Cherry Hills (Book 14)
Valentine's in Cherry Hills (Book 15)
Drowned in Cherry Hills (Book 16)
Orphaned in Cherry Hills (Book 17)
Fatal Fête in Cherry Hills (Book 18)
Arson in Cherry Hills (Book 19)
Overdosed in Cherry Hills (Book 20)
Trapped in Cherry Hills (Book 21)
Missing in Cherry Hills (Book 22)
Crash in Cherry Hills (Book 23)
Independence Day in Cherry Hills (Book 24)
Checked Out in Cherry Hills (Book 25)
Blackmail in Cherry Hills (Book 26)
Last Supper in Cherry Hills (Book 27)

Slain in Cherry Hills (Book 28)
Clean Kill in Cherry Hills (Book 29)
Targeted in Cherry Hills (Book 30)
Due or Die in Cherry Hills (Book 31)
Recalled in Cherry Hills (Book 32)
Arrested in Cherry Hills (Book 33)
Bad Blood in Cherry Hills (Book 34)
Burglary in Cherry Hills (Book 35)

Psychic Poker Pro Mystery Series:
Murder in the Cards (Book 1)

POISONED *in* CHERRY HILLS

PAIGE SLEUTH

ISBN: 1518810357
ISBN-13: 978-1518810350

Published by Marla Bradeen.

CHAPTER ONE

"Those two have trouble written all over them," Imogene Little said. The petite fifty-something's mouth was pinched as she looked across the adoption room set up as part of the Furry Friends Foster Families benefit dinner.

Katherine Harper's gaze followed the direction of Imogene's. Two twenty-something women, a redhead and a blonde, stood arguing in the cat corner. The redhead leaned in the blonde's face, her cheeks flushed and her arms jerking about. A tabby in the cage behind her had stretched one paw as far as it would go through the bars in order to swat at her swinging ponytail.

"I hope their antics don't get us booted from the Cherry Hills Hotel after they were nice enough to donate space for tonight's event," Imogene said. "Then they'll never want to deal with 4F again."

Two chihuahuas circled around the women's feet, yapping as if to referee the disagreement. The dogs weren't the only creatures who noticed the tension heating up on the other side of the room. Kat would be surprised if anyone in attendance hadn't gotten wind of it. Several men in the nearby vicinity had even leaned against the walls as if settling in to watch a choreographed performance put on as part of the night's entertainment.

"What are they arguing about?" Kat asked, hoping they were in a bidding war over one of the animals present. Between the dozen or so dogs, twenty cats, and one lone rabbit being showcased this evening, the more people who showed an interest in adopting one of the animals, the more of a success tonight's event would be.

Imogene groaned, apparently not sharing Kat's optimism. "Knowing them, a man."

Kat turned toward her. "You know them?"

Imogene nodded. "Lucy Callahan and Heidi

Smith have lived here since they were teenagers. Even then they didn't get along. They both seem to go for the same type, and inevitably somebody's heart ends up getting broken."

Kat frowned at the mention of men. Sneaking a peek at the wall clock, she wondered where her own date was. Hopefully Andrew Milhone hadn't gotten caught up at work. Being a police detective, he often kept erratic hours.

Of course, Kat had to remind herself, calling tonight's outing a 'date' wasn't entirely accurate. Although she had already elevated it to that level in her mind, she wasn't sure whether Andrew shared her sentiments. For all she knew, in his mind they were just two childhood friends going out to support the homeless animals of Cherry Hills, Washington. Otherwise, wouldn't he have called to let her know he'd be running late?

An angry shout redirected Kat's attention to the problem developing across the room. "Should we intervene?" she asked Imogene.

"Other than asking them to leave, I'm not sure what we can do. We might have to let them battle it out for a while longer. But help me monitor the situation. The last thing we need is a brouhaha ruining tonight for everybody else."

"I'll keep an eye on them," Kat assured her friend.

"Thank you." Imogene took a step backward. "Well, I suppose I ought to go circulate like a good hostess. I'll talk to you later."

"Okay."

As Imogene wandered off, a large, yellow Labrador Retriever trotted up to Kat and stuck his head up her dress with enough force to send her wobbling in her stiletto heels. Thankfully, she regained her footing in time to keep from flashing the room, using the dog to steady herself.

"Sorry 'bout that," a tall, thin brunette said, pulling on the leash attached to the dog's collar while trying to maintain her hold on a sparkly clutch bag. She gave the leash another tug, but the dog gave no indication that he'd felt it. "I didn't expect Champ to be such a handful."

"It's okay," Kat said, stroking Champ's head. He gazed adoringly up at her with soulful brown eyes.

"He looked so despondent in his pen I thought I'd just walk him around for a little while to cheer him up. It turns out he's walking me more than I am him."

Kat tilted her head. "Are you thinking about

adopting him?"

The woman hugged her purse a little tighter. "Oh, I don't know. It's such a big commitment, caring for another living creature."

"It is," Kat concurred, "but it can also be very rewarding."

The woman regarded her. "Do you have any pets?"

"Yes, two cats." Kat couldn't help but smile as she thought of her beloved felines. "They find new ways to amuse me every day."

As if he was determined to prove that his entertainment value exceeded anything a cat could provide, Champ sat on his haunches and flapped his front paws, reminding Kat of a seal. Both women laughed as they watched him.

"Have you ever had a dog before?" Kat asked.

The woman shook her head, her shoulders sagging a little. "My fiancé never liked animals in the house."

Kat didn't say anything. From the way the woman choked on the word 'fiancé,' she figured he was no longer in the picture.

"I'm Tasha Taylor, by the way," the woman said.

"Kat Harper."

"It's nice to meet you." Tasha wedged her clutch under one armpit in order to get a better grip on Champ's leash. "Maybe I will look into adopting him. Now that I'm all by myself, it makes no sense to live in that big, empty house alone."

Kat's heart warmed at the thought of another animal finding a permanent home. "I'd be happy to help arrange the paperwork if you do decide to take him. I'm one of the 4F board members."

"I'll keep that in mind."

A yell drew their attention to the other side of the room. Kat expected to see one of the over-exuberant canines in the center of the commotion, but instead she saw Lucy and Heidi. The redhead had her feet planted in a battle stance, her fists jammed on her hips as she leaned within an inch of the blonde's face.

"I wonder what that's about," Tasha said.

Kat suppressed a groan. "Tasha, would you excuse me?"

Tasha didn't look at her, her gaze transfixed on the scene across the room. "Sure. It was nice meeting you."

Kat threaded her way through the room, squeezing by several dogs and more than several dinner attendees. The dogs jumped at her with enthusiasm, overstimulated by all the activity. The humans in attendance didn't seem to be much better behaved, Kat observed as she watched the redhead shake her finger in front of the blonde's nose. Kat held her breath, fully expecting the woman to get one of her knuckles bitten off.

Fortunately, Kat arrived before the women could escalate to physical violence. "Hi there," she greeted, pretending she hadn't just stepped into the middle of a heated argument. "I'm Kat Harper. I don't believe we've met yet."

The two women glowered at each other for a moment longer before the blonde broke eye contact. She turned toward Kat, although she didn't return her smile. "Heidi Smith," she said.

The other woman—who could only be Lucy Callahan—sneered. "Take my advice, Kat, and avoid Heidi at all costs."

Kat had hoped her mere presence would turn the conversation to more neutral topics, but that apparently had been wishful thinking on her part. "Is there a problem here?" she asked, rotating her gaze between Lucy and Heidi.

Heidi folded her arms across her chest and

jutted her chin in Lucy's direction. "The only problem is her."

Lucy scoffed. "Please. You're the one who insists on following me around everywhere." She looked pointedly around the room. "Isn't there somewhere else you can go stand?"

"I'm only over here because this is where the cats are," Heidi replied.

Kat brightened. "Oh, you're looking to adopt?"

Heidi nodded. "If I find one that seems like a good fit."

Lucy snorted. "She means she wants a black cat to go with her broom and witch's hat. Halloween is only two months away, you know."

Heidi gave Lucy a withering look.

Kat cleared her throat. "Well, we have almost twenty cats currently up for adoption. Perhaps we could discuss your lifestyle and temperament requirements to find you a good match."

"Her lifestyle consists of poaching on other people's boyfriends," Lucy piped up. "In fact, I don't believe you've ever managed to snag a man without stealing him from somebody else, have you, Heidi?"

Heidi ignored her, choosing instead to focus

on Kat. "I'd be happy to discuss these animals with you before the night is over. Right now though, I need some fresh air."

Kat forced her lips up into a smile. "I understand. Come find me when you're ready."

"Good riddance," Lucy called out as Heidi walked away.

Kat watched Heidi retreat, noting the way she kept her shoulders folded inward as if shutting out her surroundings. Kat sensed a sadness about her and found herself torn between going after her to offer some comfort and staying put to keep Lucy from hunting her down and making her life more miserable. She didn't know which of the women had started tonight's hostilities or what exactly their man problems were, but, based on the short interaction she'd seen, Lucy seemed to be the instigator.

When Heidi disappeared from view, Kat twisted back around to give Lucy her full attention. The tabby that had been playing with Lucy's ponytail earlier reached a paw through the bars again, prompting Kat to smile.

"It looks like you have an admirer," she said.

Lucy visibly perked up, her eyes darting around the room.

"I mean behind you," Kat clarified, pointing.

Lucy rotated around to peer at the tabby, her features softening a fraction. "That one is pretty cute."

"All adoption fees are half off tonight," Kat encouraged.

Lucy frowned. "I'd really love to take him, but my place doesn't allow pets."

"Oh, that's too bad." Kat silently questioned why Lucy was hovering in the cat corner if that were the case. Had she chosen this spot only to pester Heidi?

"It sucks," Lucy said. "But I've been thinking about moving. Maybe once I've found a new place I can come back for him, if he's still available."

Kat's brain kicked into gear. She was determined to do what she could to find homes for the felines. "My building has vacancies, and they allow pets."

Lucy's eyes brightened. "Really?"

Kat nodded. "I live in Cherry Hills Commons, and I know of at least three empty units at the moment. If you're serious about moving, you shouldn't have any problems renting one of them."

Lucy tapped her chin. The belligerence she'd displayed earlier had completely disappeared now. "I'll have to look into that. What's the address?"

Kat gave it to her, then caught the tabby's eye. She swore the feline winked.

Kat smiled. With any luck, the tabby would soon have a permanent home.

She only hoped Lucy was kinder to animals than she had been to Heidi Smith.

CHAPTER TWO

"Kat, we have a crisis," Imogene said, swooping toward Kat not one minute after Kat had found her designated seat in the dining area.

Kat stood up. "What is it?"

Willow Wu halted right behind Imogene, a pained expression distorting the Asian American's features. "It's my fault for seating them together. I didn't know they had a history between them."

Imogene patted her hand. "How could you possibly know? Their bad blood goes back years before you moved to town."

"Who are you talking about?" Kat asked.

"Why, Lucy Callahan and Heidi Smith, of

course," Imogene said, as if they were the only two women with a rivalry in Cherry Hills.

Willow grimaced. "I ended up assigning them to the same dinner table."

Kat's stomach lurched. She couldn't imagine Lucy and Heidi's behavior magically improving over dinner.

Imogene wrung her hands. "If only we'd noticed before I made the announcement that the dining room was opening up."

Kat had to silently agree as she watched the mob of people filing into the room to locate their table number and place setting. Many of tonight's guests had already shaken out their cloth napkins or sipped from the water and iced tea glasses set out at every seat.

"Did Lucy or Heidi come with anybody else?" Kat asked.

Willow nodded. "Heidi's here with her sister, Rebecca."

"Then why don't Andrew and I switch places with them?" Kat suggested.

Imogene grasped Kat's wrist as if clinging to a lifeline. "Really? You wouldn't mind?"

Kat shook her head, wiggling out of Imogene's grip. "Andrew's not even here yet, and I haven't touched my setting. I'll just flag him over to the right table when he arrives."

Imogene rubbed her palms together. "Oh, that would be marvelous! You're an absolute lifesaver!"

Kat shrugged, shifting self-consciously as Imogene gazed at her with something approaching hero worship. She really didn't think her idea was all that novel.

Imogene touched Willow's arm. "Why don't you go intercept Heidi and Rebecca before they settle in? I'll lead Kat to her new table."

Willow nodded and rushed off.

Imogene shuffled sideways, motioning for Kat to follow. "Come along."

They pushed their way through the dining room, stopping only briefly to greet several of the other guests. Imogene seemed to know everyone in the room, which slowed down their progress despite how she tried to deflect all the attempts to engage her in conversation.

When they'd successfully maneuvered through the crowd, Imogene aimed her finger at one of the tables. "There you are. And, luckily enough, both of the Smiths' place settings look untouched."

Lucy, who was already seated, twisted around. "Imogene, you're just the person I wanted to see. I need to talk to you about this." Lucy jabbed a finger at Heidi's name printed in scrolling font on the place setting to her left.

"That's already been taken care of," Imogene chirped. She rested her hand on Kat's forearm. "Kat and her date will be switching seats with Becca and Heidi."

Lucy exhaled. "Thank goodness. And here I thought I'd have to sit next to that man-stealer all night long. Do you know what the first thing she said to me this evening was?"

Kat's heart sank. She had anticipated this evening being filled with pleasant conversation, but apparently that wasn't going to happen.

Lucy folded her arms across her chest, her eyes flashing. "She had the nerve to ask where my boyfriend was, like she wanted to rub it in that I didn't have a date. But I'll have you know, I *chose* to come alone tonight. To tell you the truth, I'm sick of men."

Imogene inched backward, looking between Kat and Lucy with a smile that didn't quite reach her eyes. "Well, I'll leave you two alone to get acquainted."

Lucy lifted her hand up and waved as Imogene scurried away.

Kat slipped into the chair originally reserved

for Rebecca Smith, leaving the seat between her and Lucy for Andrew. She felt a bit guilty about her plan to use him as a conversational buffer, then exonerated herself with the reminder that *he* was the one who had opted to show up late.

But to her dismay, the empty chair between them did nothing to deter Lucy. She leaned across it and said, “Let me tell you about my last boyfriend, Kyle, and how Heidi turned him against me.” She snorted. “You’re going to love this.”

Kat swallowed and resisted the urge to look at the clock. Next time, she would think twice before she volunteered to switch places with someone else at dinner.

CHAPTER THREE

"So, what'd I miss?" Andrew Milhone asked Kat, sliding into the empty seat between her and Lucy.

Kat groaned. "For starters, a heated debate between your neighbor on the right and Heidi Smith." She kept her voice low so Lucy couldn't overhear.

Andrew stole a glance at Lucy before spinning back around. He hunched closer and adopted Kat's same conspiratorial tone. "What were they arguing about?"

"Men."

He grinned. "There just aren't enough of us to go around, huh?"

Kat made a face. "According to Imogene,

they've been fighting over guys for years."

"In that case, maybe they'll put on another performance before the night is over."

Kat certainly hoped not, but, judging from the way Andrew's eyes had lit up, he wasn't opposed to personally witnessing a catfight any more than the other males in attendance. She would have expected better from a member of the Cherry Hills Police Department. Hadn't he seen enough scuffles during his ten years on the force to have grown tired of them by now?

Andrew set one hand on Kat's knee. "You look nice, by the way."

The heat from his palm shot up her leg and zipped through every cell in her body like an electric current. All thoughts of Lucy and Heidi dissipated into the air surrounding them. "Thank you." She took in his crisp, gray, button-down shirt and black slacks. "So do you."

"You didn't see me an hour ago. I could have arrived a little earlier, but felt compelled to shower and change so nobody would mistake me for one of your homeless dogs."

"You looked that bad, huh?"

He smirked. "I refuse to answer that."

"What happened to you anyway?"

Andrew pulled his hand away and reached

for the iced tea in front of him. "I got held up at work."

Kat adjusted her dress. Her knee was still tingling where Andrew had rested his hand. "Anything serious?"

"Nah, just some paperwork related to a case we closed recently. Chief wanted my final report filed by the end of the day."

"He sounds like a real slave driver."

Andrew laughed. "Not really. He basically just didn't want to be held liable when the pile of papers on my desk finally toppled over and ended up suffocating one of the other officers."

Andrew's amusement was infectious, and Kat couldn't prevent her own giggle from escaping.

Andrew looked her up and down, his penetrating blue eyes sending a little tremor through her body. "If I had known how amazing you look, I would have pulled the fire alarm so Chief would have no choice but to let me leave early."

The compliment caused Kat to blush. She slipped her hands into her lap, resisting the temptation to push back a lock of sandy hair that had fallen over Andrew's forehead.

Andrew coughed and surveyed the room. "Did you order already?"

Kat nodded, eyeing one of the servers distributing entrées. "You missed the soup and salad, but I told them to bring you a main course."

"What did you choose for me?"

"The cassava with sofrito."

"Sounds good."

The corners of her mouth twitched. "You have no idea what that is, do you?"

"Nope," he agreed cheerfully. "But I'll find out when it gets here."

She laughed. It still amazed her that she had never noticed how attractive Andrew was when they were growing up. She supposed she was so anxious to get out of Cherry Hills after she graduated high school fifteen years ago that a possible romance had never even entered her mind. But ever since her return to town a month ago, she hadn't been able to think about anything but what a good catch her old childhood friend was.

She only wished she knew whether her feelings were mutual.

"Hey," Lucy piped up from Andrew's other side. "You're a cop, aren't you?"

"That I am." Andrew held out his hand. "Andrew Milhone."

"Lucy." She scooted closer to him as they shook hands. "Tell me, Andrew Milhone, why isn't it illegal when a tramp steals another woman's boyfriend?"

Kat stilled as she caught sight of the coy smile that Lucy flashed at Andrew. Was she hitting on him? What had happened to her being sick of men?

"Probably a matter of budget constraints." Andrew chuckled. "You know how big a force we'd need if breaking hearts was deemed a punishable offense?"

Lucy tapped her chin, as though seriously reflecting on his comment. "True enough." She dropped her elbows on the table. "But there should still be a law against certain behavior. I mean, we live in a civilized society, ya know?"

"Well, I can tell you that kidnapping a potential love interest against their will is illegal."

Kat frowned, wondering if she were misreading Andrew's playful tone. The thought of him flirting back with Lucy Callahan twisted her insides into a knot. She pretended to adjust her napkin in her lap to mask her discomfort.

Lucy leaned closer and propped her chin on her hands. "If your department is open to suggestions, I have a few ideas on what you could do to lower the crime rate in Cherry Hills. As this town gets bigger, safety concerns will only increase."

Andrew rotated sideways to give her his undivided attention. "I'm all ears."

Kat gritted her teeth and sat on her hands so she wouldn't be tempted to tug on Andrew's sleeve like a petulant child. She wished now that she *had* taken the seat right next to Lucy.

Lucy sat up straighter. "Okay, so, CHPD can only employ so many officers, right? That means it's really up to us citizens to do our part. What I've been thinking is . . ."

Kat slumped in her seat as Lucy launched into a speech about recruiting the public to form neighborhood watch associations. From the way she batted her eyelashes every so often, Kat suspected she'd only brought up the proposal in the hopes that she and Andrew could spearhead the initiative together, giving her an excuse to see him regularly.

Kat sighed, mentally berating herself for being so uncharitable. Naturally Lucy wouldn't see anything wrong with chatting up the handsome, single man occupying the chair next to her. When they'd been talking before his arrival, Kat had deliberately emphasized that she and

Andrew were just two good friends out to show their support for homeless animals. She hadn't brought up her attraction to him, fearful that Lucy might let something slip to Andrew himself.

Now, though, Kat was starting to regret not opening up more. Maybe if she'd dropped even a tiny hint about her romantic interest in Andrew, Lucy wouldn't be hoarding all of his attention.

A piercing scream penetrated Kat's thoughts and nearly caused her to lose all bladder control. Beside her, Lucy and Andrew abruptly stopped talking, both of their heads whipping toward the source of the scream.

Kat spun around a split second after they did. An older, chestnut-haired woman stood by one of the tables, her hands clamped over her mouth.

The room had fallen completely silent. Everyone was too busy staring at the woman to continue with their own conversations. Several people had started to approach her, concern etched across their faces.

Among the people moving closer, Kat spotted Imogene. When Imogene arrived at the source of the commotion, she crouched down, disappearing for a few seconds before jumping back up.

"We need a doctor," she yelled.

A man Kat recognized as a local veterinarian stepped forward. "What's the problem?"

The woman who had screamed dropped her hands to her sides, exposing her ashen face. She didn't raise her voice, but she didn't have to. Kat could hear her clearly in the eerie silence of the dining room.

"Heidi Smith collapsed. I—I think she might be dead."

CHAPTER FOUR

Although Andrew had yet to return to their table, Kat had already heard the rampant speculation circulating among the guests. As quiet as the room had been earlier, now it seemed as though no one could stop chattering.

The veterinarian who had rushed forward to assist had verified that Heidi Smith was indeed dead. Nobody was quite sure what had happened yet, but the guesses ranged from her having a heart attack to someone deliberately taking her life. Andrew had joined the fray soon afterward, perhaps already suspecting his services as police detective would be required.

It wasn't long afterward that he announced no one could leave until the police determined exactly what was going on, and the forced confinement had generated a general air of anxiety. Despite the instructions they'd been given, nobody wanted to remain seated. Many of the guests roamed around the room, and the ones who stayed in their chairs fidgeted with restless energy. Nobody seemed to be looking forward to being interviewed as a potential witness.

All of the police activity led Kat to believe Heidi's death was most likely the result of foul play. Besides, Heidi had been young. The odds of a twenty-something-year-old woman dropping dead without warning had to be slim.

The question was, exactly what—and who—had killed her?

Kat snuck a peek at Lucy Callahan, who kept craning her neck to get a better view of the activity across the room. Kat couldn't help but remember the redhead's angry scowl as she'd faced down Heidi earlier. Could the two women really dislike each other so much that one would murder the other? The idea turned Kat's stomach.

"Can you see what's happening?" Lucy asked.

Kat shook her head, hoping to deter a lengthy conversation by remaining mute.

Lucy practically climbed on top of the table for a better view. "I'm sure Andrew will fill us in when he comes back."

Kat flinched at Lucy's use of Andrew's first name. Although, she reasoned, her familiarity only made sense. After all, the two had met before the dining room had become a potential crime scene, before Andrew had morphed into Detective Milhone of the Cherry Hills Police Department.

Lucy straightened. "He's coming this way."

Kat scanned the area, her heart beating a little faster when she saw that Andrew was indeed headed toward them. He halted next to their table, his face grim.

"You all are up next," he said, glancing in turn at the five people seated around the table. "I'll be escorting you one at a time to another room so I or one of my colleagues can interview you in private. Once we've captured your statement, you're free to leave."

"Can you give us an update?" Lucy said, bouncing in her seat. "What's going on?"

Andrew's mouth thinned. "Heidi didn't make it. Right now, we're suspecting foul play. Our best guess at this time is that she was poisoned, but we've expedited some samples to the lab for confirmation."

Lucy's mouth dropped open. Kat couldn't tell whether she found the news more shocking or exciting.

Andrew's eyes didn't leave Lucy's face. "Why don't I start with you? You seem to have known the victim better than most everybody else here."

"Sure." Lucy scrambled to stand up.

Kat leaned back in her seat and fanned herself with one hand as Andrew led Lucy away. She closed her eyes to block out the dizzying swarm of activity around her but still couldn't prevent the slightly nauseated feeling that had been building in her gut for the past twenty minutes.

Figuring she had enough time to splash some water on her face before Andrew returned to take her away for questioning, Kat slipped her purse strap over her shoulder, stood up, and made her way toward the restrooms.

Crossing the hotel corridor, Kat flung the bathroom door open and strode inside. But before she could reach the sink, the sight of Champ standing guard by the garbage can stopped her short.

The Labrador's ears pricked, and he rushed

forward to look up her dress again. However, this time Kat was expecting the ambush and managed to turn away in time.

As she stroked Champ, Kat heard the unmistakable sound of someone retching from behind a closed stall door. She wasn't surprised that the shock of this evening's turn of events had made at least one person sick. Kat's own stomach wouldn't stop roiling either.

The toilet flushed and the door banged open. Tasha Taylor stepped out, halting when she saw Kat. "Oh, you startled me," she said, gripping her clutch purse close to her chest. "I didn't realize anybody else was in here."

Kat's heart pinched in sympathy as she took in Tasha's pale face and the mascara trails streaking down her cheeks. "Are you okay?"

"Yes. No. Not really." Tasha leaned against the side of the stall, pressing her hand against her stomach. "This whole thing with Heidi is just really upsetting."

"Did you know her?"

Tasha sucked in a breath as she bobbed her head.

"It's terrible what happened," Kat said.

"Yes." Tasha stumbled over to the sink and rinsed out her mouth.

Champ whimpered and trotted over to Tasha. He pressed the top of his head into her palm as if sensing her need for comfort. After a moment, she rubbed his ears.

Watching the two interacting with such affection would have infused Kat with cheer under normal circumstances, but her heart was too heavy at the moment.

"I'm guessing he's in here because you decided to adopt him," she said.

Tasha glanced at the dog. "Yeah, I couldn't resist."

"You won't regret it," Kat assured her.

Tasha bent over to grab Champ's leash. When she straightened, her eyes were red and watery, as though she were on the verge of crying again. "Well, I should be heading home. After talking to the police, I'm beat."

"Okay," Kat said. "I enjoyed meeting you, despite how things turned out."

Tasha grabbed a paper towel and swiped at her tear-stained face before depositing the towel in the garbage and taking a giant step toward the door. "Bye."

As soon as Tasha left, Kat approached the sink and turned on the tap. Dipping her fingers under the stream of cool water, she patted some onto her face, feeling instantly better. When she finished, she leaned against the counter, in no rush to return to the dining room. The silence of the bathroom made it easier for her to think about Heidi.

The more she considered it, the less likely it seemed that Lucy could be responsible for what had happened. Although there certainly was no love lost between the two women, Lucy hadn't left their table since Kat had sat down. When would she have found the opportunity to kill Heidi?

Then again, if Heidi had been poisoned, it was possible whatever she'd ingested hadn't taken effect right away. Could Lucy have slipped her something earlier that evening only for Heidi to drop dead hours later?

Kat sighed. She should leave the investigating to Andrew. And she really needed to get back to her table before Andrew began to wonder if she'd snuck off.

After studying herself in the mirror to make sure she looked presentable, Kat yanked a paper towel out of the dispenser and dried her hands. When she went to toss the sheet, something poking out from underneath one of the wadded-up towels in the garbage can caught her eye. She reached down and picked it up.

Kat turned her find around in her fingers, her heart beating a little faster as she inspected the small vial. The vial was clearly empty and there wasn't any label to indicate what it had held, but her mind had already turned in a sinister direction. She could easily picture this tiny container holding enough poison to kill a woman.

The possibility sent a shiver down Kat's spine.

Careful not to touch more of the vial's surface area than she needed to, Kat wrapped it in a clean paper towel and slipped it into her purse. She would turn it over to Andrew when it was her turn to be questioned. Then, she vowed, she would step back and let him handle the difficult part of determining who had killed Heidi Smith.

CHAPTER FIVE

"Ugh, what a disaster," Imogene said, slumping against one of the adoption room walls. "When I saw tonight's benefit dinner unfolding in my head, I envisioned it ending with everybody eating cake, not poor Heidi's death and a police interrogation."

Imogene slid down the wall and buried her face in her hands. Almost immediately, two medium-sized mutts bounded over to administer emergency aid in the form of slobbery tongues lapping at her face with enthusiastic vigor.

Imogene giggled before rising to her feet again. "Okay, okay. You've successfully cheered me up!"

Kat wanted to slump to the floor herself. After the stress of the benefit dinner, she felt as if all the energy had been drained from her body.

The police interviews had lasted for several hours, and most of the guests couldn't get out of the door fast enough once they'd been cleared to leave. But, unfortunately, ducking out early hadn't been an option for the three members of the Furry Friends Foster Families board. They still had to clean up and put everything back in order.

On the bright side, all but five of the homeless animals had been adopted.

Imogene rubbed the dogs' bellies while they rolled around at her feet. "I can't believe you two didn't find homes tonight."

"They will," Willow said, folding up an empty pen that had once contained one of the luckier dogs. "It's just a matter of time."

"You're right," Imogene agreed. "With personalities as big as these two's, they won't be homeless forever."

Kat eyed the cat corner as she wandered around the adoption room picking up debris and stuffing it into a garbage bag. "I don't remember seeing Clover tonight," she said, referring to Imogene's current foster. "Did he find a home already?"

Imogene flushed. "Yes, you could say that. I decided to adopt him myself."

Kat grinned. After watching her friend interacting with the big, white feline, she wasn't surprised. "I knew you wouldn't be able to give him up."

"Nope, you were right about that." Imogene's eyes twinkled. "I notice Tom wasn't here either."

"I kind of decided to adopt him permanently too," Kat admitted, thinking of the beautiful brown-and-black cat she'd taken in as a foster not too long ago. "He gets along so well with Matty that she would be heartbroken if he went to live somewhere else."

"I bet." Imogene smirked, clearly aware that Kat's own affections toward Tom were more than a little responsible for her decision to keep him.

Kat frowned as a meow sounded from inside one of the cages. "Weren't the foster parents supposed to take any unadopted animals home with them after the event ended?"

"I offered to bring them back once I finished up here," Imogene said. "I couldn't see any sense in our volunteers having to linger around after their police interviews, and the police didn't want anything—including the animals—removed from the premises until they had a chance to look over the property for evidence."

Kat nodded, remembering the vial she'd found in the women's room. Andrew had promised to send it to the crime lab for testing ASAP.

"Do you want help transporting the animals to their foster families?" Kat asked.

Imogene brightened. "That would be marvelous. You can handle the cats' return, if you'd like."

"Okay. Who's fostering the cats?"

"Tabitha the tabby is being cared for by Pauline Brooks," Willow piped up. "She lives in my neighborhood, so I can take Tabitha when we leave. The Belleroses have the Siamese and the black cat."

Kat paused from scooping up garbage. "The Belleroses were sitting at Heidi's table, weren't they?" She recalled seeing the unusual last name printed on the place setting next to her before she had switched seats.

"Yes," Willow confirmed.

Imogene shook her head. "Those poor souls. Bob's heart is already weak. It's a miracle he didn't go into cardiac arrest when Heidi dropped dead in front of them."

"The Belleroses almost seemed more agitated about Heidi than Rebecca," Willow added.

"That's because poor Becca is in shock." Imogene tsked. "We're going to have to do something for her. Heidi's death must be a terrible blow, particularly after what happened with their parents."

"What happened with their parents?" Kat asked.

Imogene set her hand over her heart. "They passed away recently."

Kat's stomach tightened. "How did they die?"

"Car accident this past winter. It was a horrible, appalling tragedy."

"What happened?" Kat asked, imagining their car losing control after skidding over a patch of black ice.

Imogene's shoulders sagged. "That's the most tragic part of it all. Jake Lobeck was drunk as a skunk, but he still had his keys on him. He plowed right into the Smiths' car on his way home from some party. Poor Heidi and Becca were still getting used to being orphans, and now this business with Heidi . . ." Imogene took a deep, shuddering breath as she trailed off.

A stone settled in Kat's gut. "That's terrible."

"It certainly was," Imogene agreed. "We definitely need to do something for her, on behalf of 4F."

"Why don't we stop by her house tomorrow afternoon?" Willow suggested. "Kat, do you have to work at Jessie's?"

"No, I have the day off."

"Good. Then we'll each make up a dish to bring over and go pay our condolences," Willow said.

"I don't think anybody will want to eat anything I cook," Kat warned.

"Pick up something from Jessie's Diner," Imogene replied. "You can't go wrong with anything on Jessie's menu."

Kat had to agree with her there. Just thinking about Jessie's decadent lasagna layered with spicy marinara sauce and mozzarella cheese made her mouth water.

Imogene planted her hands on her hips, her mouth set in a determined line as she surveyed the room. "Well, I suppose we ought to get a move on and whip this place into shape so we can skedaddle on out of here. I'm ready to go home, throw on some pj's, and unwind."

"I second that," Willow said.

"Clover is going to be miffed I've stayed out this late," Imogene said.

Willow's mouth curved up. "He'll still be happy to see you. I've never seen a cat more in love with his mistress."

Imogene beamed. "The feeling is mutual."

Kat's thoughts wandered to her own two cats. Although Matty wasn't too keen on open displays of affection, she had her own, quiet way of letting Kat know how content she was to have her as a human.

Tom, on the other hand, loved to soak up as much attention as he could, and he wasn't shy about begging for it. He'd only been with Kat for a short time, but he had already taken to greeting her at the front door when she returned home and snuggling against her when she went to bed. Kat couldn't believe she'd once tried to talk herself out of adopting the big feline. Now, she would be devastated to lose him.

Just thinking about being reunited with her cats infused her with new resolve. She shook out her garbage bag and returned to work.

CHAPTER SIX

The Belleroses' two foster cats meowed unhappily from their prison in the back seat during the drive home. Kat tuned them out, preoccupied by Heidi's death. She couldn't help but wonder if the Belleroses had seen anything to help identify the person who had killed Heidi. Sitting so close to the Smiths during dinner, they were both prime candidates to have observed anything suspicious.

Kat shook her head as she pulled into the Belleroses' driveway, reminding herself that catching the killer wasn't her responsibility. Andrew had been put in charge of the case, and he was more than competent at his job.

Still, she reasoned, she should do what she

could to uncover the truth, considering that she served on the board of the organization that had put on tonight's event. And would it really hurt for her to inquire a little while she was here? It wasn't as if she were going out of her way to interview the Belleroses.

She took a deep breath and climbed out of the car. After she unbuckled the cat carrier, she tottered carefully toward the house, hoping she didn't trip in her heels. Luckily, she made it without incident, and, between juggling her car keys and maintaining her hold on the cat carrier, she somehow managed to ring the doorbell.

Several sharp barks sounded from inside. In addition to fostering two cats, the Belleroses apparently had their own dog too.

The door swung open, revealing a portly elderly man with a pale complexion and a wide smile. "Welcome. You must be Kat."

"Yes, hi."

He moved aside so she could enter. "Willow called and told me to expect you. I'm Bob Belle-rose."

"Nice to meet you."

Kat stepped into the sitting area, recognizing the older brunette on the sofa as the one who had screamed after Heidi had collapsed. Tasha Taylor sat next to her. Both of them still wore their party dresses, although they'd sloughed off their heels in favor of going barefoot.

"Hi, Kat," Tasha said.

"Hi."

Kat wondered what Tasha was doing here, but before she could ask Champ came tearing down the hallway, his nails clicking on the hardwood floors. He welcomed Kat with a snuffle up her dress that sent her keys clattering to the floor.

Tasha jumped off the couch and grabbed hold of Champ's collar. "Stop that!" She smiled ruefully at Kat. "Sorry. He seems to like you."

Kat shifted her legs in an attempt to realign her dress without dropping the cats. "It's okay."

"I was just telling Tasha that Bob and I would be more than willing to give her some advice on how to train him to behave a bit better," the brunette said. "The last thing we need is Champ wandering onto our property and tearing up my garden."

Tasha ran her hands over the Labrador's head. "I'm fortunate to live next door to people who know so much about animals. I've never had a dog before, and, I have to admit, I'm feeling a little overwhelmed at the moment."

The brunette covered Tasha's hand with hers. "Don't worry, you'll learn soon enough. Comfort comes from experience. When you've fostered as many animals as we have, you're bound to pick up a few pointers."

"Lucky me," Tasha replied.

The woman turned back to Kat. "I'm Meg Bellerose, by the way."

"Kat. Nice to meet you."

Meg stood up and reached for the cats. "I see you've come to reunite us with our charges."

Kat handed over the carrier. "Sorry to say they were two of the few who didn't find homes tonight."

"Oh, they will. This duo is too personable for somebody not to snatch them up."

Champ sprinted over and pressed his nose against the carrier. His tail wagged nonstop despite the fierce hisses prompted by his greeting.

Meg gently pushed the Labrador away. "I'm afraid these little critters might find you a bit intimidating, Champ."

Tasha slipped her shoes back on and stood up. "I should probably take him home. It's getting late."

Meg set the carrier on the floor and gave Tasha a hug. "Take care of yourself."

"Thanks." Tasha grabbed Champ's leash off the coffee table and clipped it onto his collar.

Meg escorted Tasha and Champ out the front door, then returned to the living room. She sprang open the carrier door before re-claiming her seat on the couch. "Why don't you sit down and join us for a while," Meg said to Kat, patting the sofa cushion next to her.

"Okay, sure." Kat hoped she didn't sound too eager as she perched next to Meg, but she wouldn't be able to let this opportunity to cajole some information about the night's events pass without regretting it later.

She stole a peek at Bob, who had quietly taken a seat on an armchair and now had his nose buried in a car magazine. She wondered if she would be able to get any information out of him without aggravating his heart condition.

But before Kat could broach the topic, Meg said, "I just feel so bad for her."

"Rebecca Smith, you mean?" Kat asked.

"Her too, but I was referring to Tasha."

"Oh."

Meg crossed her legs, watching as one of the cats poked her nose out of the carrier. "I know she's lonely, which is why she adopted a dog."

Seeing no sign of Champ, the Siamese stepped out and padded off to the kitchen. The black cat quickly followed.

"Of course, nobody could blame her for being hesitant to love again, not after what happened," Meg went on.

"What happened?" Kat asked.

Meg's eyebrows crept up her forehead as though she were surprised by Kat's failure to keep up with the town's latest gossip. "Her fiancé was just sentenced to prison."

Kat felt her jaw slipping open and hastily righted it. When Tasha had mentioned a former fiancé earlier, Kat had envisioned a breakup being the cause of their separation, not a jail sentence.

"Jake was convicted of vehicular homicide," Meg said.

"That's terrible."

"Yes, it was. And not just for Tasha, but for those poor Smith girls as well."

Kat recalled the story Imogene had told her earlier, mentally slotting the pieces together. "Tasha's fiancé was the drunk driver who killed the Smiths?"

"Yes," Meg confirmed. "So sad for everyone

involved. Tasha lost the love of her life, and those Smith girls lost their parents."

A physical ache spread throughout Kat's chest. Although she herself had grown up in foster care and had never known her parents, Heidi and Rebecca Smith's heartbreak was all too easy to envision.

Meg shook her head. "And now Heidi's gone too. I wouldn't blame Becca if she needed counseling after this."

Sensing her opening, Kat shifted to face Meg better. "You were sitting next to the Smith sisters during the benefit dinner, weren't you?"

Meg nodded. "Such wonderful girls, both of them. I don't know who would do something so awful to poor Heidi."

"By chance, did you see anything suspicious this evening?"

"No, nothing." Meg fingered the hem of her dress. "And I feel so guilty about that too."

Bob cleared his throat. "You couldn't have known what was going to happen, Meg."

Meg sat up a little straighter. "But I should have been paying more attention."

Bob spread his hands, as if to reiterate she wasn't at fault.

Meg collapsed against the sofa with a sigh,

her eyes on Kat. "I told Detective Andrew I would sleep on it and call him if I remembered more later, but I doubt I'll have anything new for him in the morning. I have to tell you, my memory isn't like it was at your age."

"Ginkgo," Bob piped up. "A daily supplement would improve your short-term memory."

Meg rolled her eyes. "You've been taking that stuff for years, and your memory is worse than mine."

"I'm also almost a decade older than you, m'dear," Bob said, winking at Kat. "Just imagine how much worse I'd be if I stopped taking the stuff."

"You didn't see anything unusual this evening either?" Kat asked Bob.

"No."

Kat acknowledged his response with a nod, trying not to feel too discouraged.

As if to comfort her, the black cat ambled over and jumped onto Kat's lap. He set his front paws flat on her dress and began kneading her thighs.

Meg chuckled. "He likes you."

In response to Meg's voice, the cat stepped over to his foster human and curled up in her lap.

Meg ran one hand down the cat's body. "I missed you, too. And don't you worry. You'll find yourself a forever mama soon enough."

Kat stood up and smoothed out her dress, longing to be reunited with her own cats. "Well, it's late, and I should be heading home."

Meg smiled at her. "Thank you for bringing the cats over."

Kat took a step toward the door, careful not to stab Meg's bare toes with one of her pencil-thin heels. "No problem. Thank you for taking care of them."

Bob set down his magazine and stood up. "I'll see you to your car."

"Okay."

"Are those your keys?" Meg interjected, aiming one finger at Kat's key chain still on the floor.

"Oh, fiddlesticks." Kat scooped her keys off the floor. "I forgot I'd dropped them."

Bob tapped the side of his head, flashing her a knowing look before uttering one word. "Ginkgo."

CHAPTER SEVEN

It was almost eleven o'clock at night when Kat finally returned to her apartment building. She barely had the energy to board the lobby elevator.

But despite the intensity of her physical exhaustion, mentally she was as alert as ever. Meg's comment about Tasha's fiancé serving time in prison had led Kat to question whether his incarceration might be related to more than just the deaths of the older Smiths. What she couldn't figure out was how their car accident could be linked to Heidi's death. The best she could come up with was that Heidi was somehow instrumental in getting the vehicular homicide charges to stick, spurring Tasha Taylor to murder her for revenge.

But that theory didn't account for why Tasha had seemed genuinely distraught when they had run into each other in the hotel restroom. If Tasha had just murdered someone whom she felt had done her wrong, wouldn't she have come across as happy or smug instead?

Kat shook the thoughts aside as she exited the elevator on the third floor. She wouldn't be able to sleep if she kept dwelling on the events of this evening.

She unlocked her apartment door, spying Matty and Tom nestled together on the couch. Just looking at them made her feel ten pounds lighter.

"You guys have the right idea," she said, yawning. She shut the door, tossed her purse on the coffee table, and kicked off her shoes.

Matty looked up briefly, then settled her head back on her paws as if she couldn't care less that Kat had made it home safely. Tom, on the other hand, stood up and stretched before jumping off the sofa and padding over to meow his greeting.

"I missed you too, buddy," Kat said, crouching down to pet him.

After giving Matty and Tom a few minutes of attention, Kat couldn't keep her head up any longer. She changed into her pajamas and was almost ready to settle into bed when her cell phone rang.

Groaning, she trudged into the living room and fished her phone out of her purse. Some of her weariness faded when she saw Andrew's name lighting up the caller ID.

She punched the button to answer and pressed the phone against her ear. "Hi."

"Hey. Did I wake you?"

The sound of his voice caused her heart to beat a little faster. "No, I just got home."

"Okay, good."

Kat sat down on the sofa. "What's up?"

"I wanted to apologize for missing so much of the dinner tonight. I didn't want you to feel abandoned."

His words warmed her insides. "It's okay. I know the circumstances were beyond your control." Her mind started churning through the possibilities again. "Do you have any leads yet?"

"No. Nobody claims to have seen anything out of the ordinary, and nobody knows who might have wanted Heidi dead—other than Lucy Callahan perhaps."

"You don't think Lucy did it?" Kat asked.

"I'm keeping an open mind."

Kat pressed her lips together. She didn't miss how he hadn't really answered her question. She didn't know if that was because he thought Lucy was innocent or because he wasn't at liberty to discuss the case with a civilian.

Deciding not to push the issue, Kat said, "Did you know Heidi?"

"Yeah." From the pain in Andrew's voice, Kat gathered he also couldn't fathom who would want to hurt her.

"This must be awful for Rebecca," Kat said.

"No doubt." He paused. "Look, do you mind if I stop by there on my way home? I'm too wound up to sleep, and you sound like you are too."

Despite the melancholy air sparked by the topic of their conversation, Kat couldn't prevent the surge of excitement generated by his words. "Sure."

"See you soon."

Kat dashed into the bedroom and exchanged her pajamas for a pair of jeans and a T-shirt. Although she wasn't quite sure yet where her relationship with Andrew was headed, they were definitely not to the point where she could comfortably sit around in her nightclothes while chatting about a woman's murder.

As soon as she reentered the living room, Matty and Tom began their nightly wrestling match. Kat found it amusing how they waited for her to return home before chasing each other around the apartment. At least, she presumed they waited for her. Given how they were both always completely conked out when she stepped through the front door, she didn't figure they burned off much energy during her absences.

Matty had just locked Tom in a stronghold and was using her hind feet to kick at his head when the doorbell rang. Kat shot off the couch and practically threw the door open.

Andrew grinned at her. "I would have buzzed, but somebody else was opening the outside door just as I arrived."

"It's okay. Come in."

He stepped inside. He still wore the same slacks and button-down shirt he'd had on earlier, but his clothes were noticeably more wrinkled now. She supposed that was to be expected when you spent all evening interviewing potential witnesses as part of a homicide investigation.

Kat shut the door and folded her hands in front of her, resisting her urge to smooth out his outfit. She was about to tell him to have a seat, but before she could voice the invitation Matty came tearing through the room, Tom at her heels. They both disappeared into the kitchen, then reappeared a second later. Matty flopped onto the carpet, and Tom pounced on top of her. They rolled around for a little while before Tom jumped up and ran back the way they'd come. This time Matty did the chasing.

Kat had to laugh at their antics, even though she'd witnessed this exact scenario every evening for the past two weeks, when Tom had come to live with them.

Andrew sat down on the sofa. "I've never seen them so rambunctious. Have you been slipping caffeine in their chow?"

"No, I'm not that generous. I keep anything caffeinated for myself."

Andrew chuckled, his eyes never leaving her face. His dimples grew more pronounced the longer he stared at her.

Kat broke her gaze away from his, feeling awkward all of a sudden. "Can I get you something to drink?"

"Sure." He propped one ankle on the opposite knee. “A scotch would be great.”

She frowned. “I don’t have any scotch.”

“Then anything alcoholic will do.”

Kat fetched him a beer, opting for water herself. Drinking this late would keep her up all night.

“Thanks,” Andrew replied, taking a swig from the bottle she handed him.

Kat settled onto the sofa opposite him. “How familiar are you with the local drunk driving cases?”

He paused mid-sip. “Are you trying to tell me something? I’ll make sure this beer has worn off before I head home.”

“No, I didn’t mean to imply anything like that,” she assured him. “I know you’re a responsible driver. I’m wondering specifically about the charges against a guy named Jake Lobeck.”

Andrew grimaced. “Oh, I’m familiar with that one. I helped put the case together for the D.A.”

Kat arched an eyebrow. “Detectives work on drunk driving cases?”

“I work on whatever I’m assigned. And since CHPD isn’t all that big, I can be assigned to pretty much anything involving the Cherry Hills force.” His brow furrowed. “But why are you asking?"

She shrugged. "I'm not sure really. I'm just curious if there could be a connection between what happened to Heidi's parents and what happened to her."

"I don't see how that's possible. Her parents' car accident was just that—an accident."

"But it was serious enough to send a man to jail," Kat pointed out.

"Yes," Andrew conceded.

"How long is Jake being put away for?"

"We built up enough charges to get him a ten-year prison term. Whether he'll serve the full sentence remains to be seen."

"And Heidi wasn't involved in his sentencing?"

"No."

"She didn't testify or anything?" Kat pressed. "She didn't vouch for what upstanding citizens her parents were or convince the jury that Jake should get the maximum for taking their lives?"

Andrew shook his head. "Nope. And there was no jury. Jake pleaded guilty, and the judge himself doled out the appropriate sentence."

Kat considered that. "So whoever killed Heidi must have disliked her for another reason."

"It would look that way. That's the angle I'm focusing on anyway."

As they lapsed into silence, Kat's gaze drifted to Matty and Tom. Both cats had calmed down and were now sprawled out on the carpet. They looked beat—exactly how Kat felt.

She looked at Andrew again. "Were you able to determine anything useful from that vial I found?"

"It's too soon to tell, but I sent it off to be tested. If any substances found inside match what the lab guys separated from the iced tea, we'll at least have a partial lead."

Kat tilted her head. "Iced tea?"

Andrew pressed his lips together, looking sheepish. "Forget I said that."

Kat gripped the edge of the couch. "I can't do that. And you can't make a comment like that then refuse to tell me what it means."

He sighed. "Fine, but this stays between us."

"My lips are sealed," she promised, pinching her thumb and index finger together and air-zipping her mouth closed.

"It was Heidi's iced tea that tested positive for the poison."

Kat absorbed that. "It would have been

fairly easy for somebody to slip something into her drink when she wasn't looking."

"Yes, and, unfortunately, I wasn't able to lift any fingerprints off the vial."

"Well, just locating it in the women's restroom gives you a bit of a clue, right?" Kat asked hopefully.

Andrew didn't look convinced. He merely shrugged one shoulder and took another sip of his beer.

Kat slouched against the sofa, trying not to get too discouraged by the lack of leads.

"Kat." Andrew set his beer aside and rested his elbows on his knees, peering at her with an intense look. "I know you have a habit of involving yourself in police investigations—"

"That's not true!" she protested.

"—but we—meaning me and the other authorities—will catch whoever did this. There's no need to put yourself in harm's way."

Kat screwed up her face. "How am I in harm's way?"

"You're not—yet. But if you start going around looking into things and sticking your nose into a murderer's business, you could be putting yourself in danger."

Kat's stubborn streak flared. But, as much

as she itched to argue, she did have to silently admit that Andrew's point was a valid one. She hadn't considered before now how getting too close to the truth might give Heidi's murderer incentive to kill her too.

Andrew slapped his palms on his thighs. "Well, I've imposed on you long enough."

"You're not imposing."

He stood up anyway. "Still, it's almost midnight. You have to be just as eager to put this day behind you as I am."

Although she couldn't disagree, his imminent departure still sparked a twinge of disappointment. "This certainly wasn't the day I was expecting to have when I woke up this morning."

"Me neither." Andrew smiled. "We'll have to arrange for a makeup dinner after I solve this case."

"Sure."

He regarded her for a long moment before saying, "I'll catch you later then."

"Okay."

After locking the door behind him, the events of the past twelve hours finally caught up to her. It took all of her remaining energy to drag herself down the hallway and into bed.

CHAPTER EIGHT

"Kat!"

The sudden shout nearly caused Kat to trip over herself as she stepped out of her apartment the next afternoon. She hadn't expected to run into anyone in the corridor, considering that she was the only building resident currently occupying the third floor. Although, now that she was recovering from the shock, she wasn't completely surprised to see the landlord and apartment manager standing before her.

"Hi, Larry," Kat said, approaching the burly, bald man. "You startled me."

"That's only because you had your head in the clouds there." Larry chuckled, then spread his hands toward the woman beside him as if showcasing a game-show prize up for grabs. "Kat Harper, meet your new neighbor, Lucy Callahan."

Lucy grinned. "Hey, neighbor."

Kat's heart skipped a beat. "You're moving in? Already?"

"Yep, thanks to your tip about the vacancies."

Kat mentally kicked herself for opening her big mouth at the benefit event. But how was she to know that Lucy would end up becoming a murder suspect an hour later?

"After everything that happened yesterday, I realized if I don't get my life in order now, I may never get the chance, ya know?" Lucy said. "I mean, when somebody you know keels over not fifty feet away, it really makes you reevaluate your own life. I've been thinking about making some changes for months. Yesterday forced me to see that if I didn't get rid of all my old baggage now I might never get the chance. Heidi's death was like a wake-up call for me."

Kat squinted at Lucy, trying to deduce whether her animated tone was the result of her new lease on life or because she no longer had to worry about her archenemy stealing another one of her boyfriends ever again.

"I heard about poor Heidi," Larry said, pursing his lips. "Rumor has it she was poisoned."

"It looks that way," Lucy agreed.

"Guy's gotta be crazy to kill a sweet gal like her."

"Who said it was a guy?" Lucy argued, leaning against the wall. "I'm banking her sister did it."

Larry screwed up his face. "Becca?"

Lucy nodded. "You know their parents died recently, right? With Heidi out of the way, she stands to inherit everything."

Kat frowned. She couldn't tell whether Lucy truly believed her proposed scenario, or if she were only trying to deflect suspicion from herself.

"Does Becca even need the money?" Larry asked. "She's a pretty successful professional gal, ain't she?"

Lucy stared at Larry as if he'd sprouted fairy wings. "Money is money. It doesn't matter how much you have, you always want more."

"All right, I'll give you that," he conceded, eyeing Kat as if he might be thinking of raising her rent.

Lucy crossed her ankles. "Besides, a man

wouldn't kill by sprinkling poison on someone's food. Haven't you noticed it's always the women who do that sort of thing?"

Kat didn't miss Lucy's reference to the food being contaminated. Was that because she wasn't aware of the toxic iced tea, or because she wanted to mask her guilt by pretending she didn't know the specifics?

"Nah," Larry said, shaking his head. "Becca doesn't have it in her to do something like that."

Lucy shrugged. "Believe what you want, but it couldn't have been fun having Heidi as a sister. And Becca was sitting right next to her, giving her opportunity as well as motive."

Lucy did have a point there, Kat admitted. Although she still had her doubts about Lucy's innocence, the fact of the matter was that Kat had yet to figure out when Lucy would have had the opportunity to slip poison into Heidi's drink.

Was it possible Lucy hadn't acted alone? Kat made a mental note to ask Andrew if he'd checked Lucy's cell phone records for calls or texts to potential accomplices.

"Hey, Kat," Larry said, pulling her back to the present. "Lucy tells me you convinced her to get a cat."

Kat raised her eyebrows. "I did?"

"Yep," Lucy concurred. "I'm going to adopt that tabby I saw yesterday. Willow will be bringing her over in a few days, after I get settled in. I'll need some pointers on how to take care of her before she arrives. Think you can help me out with that?"

"Yeah, sure," Kat replied absently. Typically the news of a homeless animal finding a permanent home would have made her ecstatic, but right now she was having trouble concentrating on anything other than Heidi's murder.

Larry clapped his palms together. "Well, I'll leave you two neighbor gals to get acquainted with one another."

Lucy waved as he headed down the corridor. "Thanks, Larry."

"If you need help carrying your furniture up, give me a holler. I'm in 1B," Larry called out, stepping into the elevator.

"Will do." Lucy turned her attention back to Kat. She smiled and raised her key up as though in toast. "Here's to fresh new starts."

Kat could barely manage a return smile.

CHAPTER NINE

Kat mulled over her recent run-in with Lucy Callahan during the drive to Rebecca Smith's house. Although Lucy hadn't seemed particularly bothered by Heidi's murder, she also wasn't giving off a guilty vibe, at least not one that Kat had detected. Or, could her satisfaction over eliminating an old rival be enough to mask any remorse she felt over taking another person's life?

Kat took a deep breath, the delicious aroma of Jessie's lasagna filling her nostrils and causing her stomach to growl. If she didn't have to keep her hands on the wheel she might be tempted to eat the whole thing herself, leaving her with nothing to offer Heidi's grieving sister.

That assumed, of course, that Rebecca really was grieving and hadn't murdered her sibling so she wouldn't have to split their parents' estate.

But Larry was right that Rebecca certainly didn't look as if she needed the money, Kat considered as she pulled up to the address Imogene had given her. The yard was immaculate, and the house's exterior didn't sport so much as a single fleck of peeling paint or a solitary gutter dent. Still, Kat couldn't overlook the possibility that maintaining appearances had driven Rebecca's savings into the ground and she was more desperate than her beautiful home would suggest.

Kat groaned, wishing she could shut off her mind. She was here to pay her respects to a woman who had just lost a close family member, she reminded herself, not to evaluate her as a murder suspect.

Imogene's car pulled up to the curb, and Imogene and Willow climbed out, both of them holding foil-covered casserole dishes. Kat got out of her own car and waited for them to catch up.

"I'm glad you're here," Kat said as they approached the house together. Not ever having met Rebecca, she had been nervous about being the first to arrive.

Imogene inhaled and depressed the doorbell. "Smells like you persuaded Jessie to make her famous lasagna."

Kat shifted the still-warm pan in her arms to keep it from singeing her skin. "She was all too willing when I told her who it was for."

The door eased open, revealing a woman who looked vaguely similar to Heidi. She shared Heidi's bone structure and blond hair, at any rate, but her eyes were red-rimmed and her nose looked ruddy from crying.

"Becca, meet Kat Harper, our new 4F treasurer," Imogene said, jerking her elbow toward Kat. "And I believe you already know Willow Wu, our secretary."

Rebecca nodded at them. "Yes, come on in."

Imogene stepped inside first, with Willow and Kat following. "We felt the least we could do was bring over some sustenance," Imogene said. "Especially after you were kind enough to agree to see us after suffering from such a terrible personal loss."

Rebecca twisted around to shut the door, obscuring her face before Kat could study it for a reaction.

Imogene bit her lip. "I must say, I feel somewhat to blame for what happened."

Rebecca faced her, her head cocked to one side. "What do you mean?"

Imogene grimaced. "As the 4F president, the benefit dinner was my responsibility."

Rebecca flapped her hand, but the motion lacked any energy behind it. "You couldn't have known."

"Nobody could," Willow said, looking pointedly at Imogene.

Imogene nodded, but the creases framing her mouth suggested she was still mentally castigating herself.

Rebecca collapsed onto the loveseat as if someone had ripped her spine out. "You can set your stuff on the coffee table."

They did, then Willow and Kat took seats on the larger couch while Imogene planted herself next to Rebecca.

Rebecca's eyes filled with tears. "I still can't believe she's gone." She snatched a tissue from the box on the end table and swiped at the corners of her eyes.

Imogene patted her hand. "We can't imagine how you must be feeling right now. To lose your only sister like that."

Rebecca blew her nose. "She was my last

remaining relative. I mean, I have some aunts and uncles and cousins, but they all live on the East Coast. I haven't seen them since Mom and Dad's funeral." She frowned. "Though I guess they'll have to fly out here again now."

"Is there anything we can do for you?" Willow asked.

Rebecca shook her head. "There's nothing anybody can do except catch the slimeball who did this."

Kat folded her hands in her lap, unable to think of anything to say that might provide even an ounce of comfort. Plus, as much as she didn't trust Lucy's judgment when it came to Heidi Smith, she also couldn't dismiss her speculation that Rebecca might be the guilty party.

Rebecca looked at Kat. "Imogene said your boyfriend is that police detective who was there last night."

Kat felt her cheeks flame. "He's not my boyfriend. But yes, we attended the benefit dinner together."

"They're good, good friends," Imogene piped up.

Rebecca hunched forward, her eyes boring into Kat's. "Does he have any guesses as to who killed her?"

"I'm not sure," Kat admitted.

Rebecca's eyes darkened. "I bet it was that tramp Lucy. I saw her and Heidi arguing before the dinner started."

Kat didn't respond, unable to fault Rebecca for her conclusion. The image of Lucy leaning against the wall of her apartment hallway while she chattered about new beginnings and old baggage flashed through her head.

Rebecca's hands balled into fists, crushing the tissue she was holding. "They've hated each other ever since they became interested in boys back in middle school. Lucy always blamed Heidi for stealing her boyfriends, but I don't know of any sane man who could spend more than a week with that shrew."

Imogene cleared her throat. "Well, I'm sure the police are conducting a thorough investigation."

Rebecca ignored her, her eyes never leaving Kat's. "Tell that detective friend of yours that I want to see justice served. I want to see Lucy Callahan behind bars before the summer is over."

"Assuming she's guilty," Imogene interjected.

Rebecca scoffed. "Of course she's guilty.

Heidi didn't have any other enemies. Nobody else had any reason to hurt her. In fact, I don't know why Lucy wasn't arrested on the spot."

Kat bit the inside of her cheek. She was tempted to ask exactly how much Rebecca had to gain financially from her sister's death, but such an insensitive inquiry was sure to get her blacklisted from not only Rebecca's social circle but quite possibly Imogene's and Willow's too.

"Did you hear me?" Rebecca said, her voice breaking into Kat's thoughts. "Tell your detective friend I demand to see justice served. I want to see Lucy pay, and I won't rest until she does."

Kat swallowed. "I'll be sure to relay your message."

Rebecca leaned back into the sofa, appearing satisfied with Kat's answer. "He's a good detective."

Kat didn't say anything, not sure where Rebecca was going.

"He helped to convict the alcoholic who killed Mom and Dad," she continued.

Imogene clucked her tongue. "Such an abysmal situation."

Rebecca tilted her head down and started

picking at her fingernails. "It was. Especially for Heidi. She used to have this passion about her, but after the accident she didn't care about anything anymore."

Imogene tsked. "It always takes some time to get over losing a loved one."

"I guess," Rebecca said, but without much conviction. "I just missed the old Heidi, you know? We used to get into these heated debates about politics and whatnot, but it was like her verve for life died when Mom and Dad did."

Kat played through her encounter with Lucy and Heidi at the 4F benefit event again. Now that she thought about it, Heidi hadn't appeared truly involved in the argument. It had been Lucy who had been ranting with enough gusto to give the illusion that both women were equally engaged.

"And now she's dead too," Rebecca went on. She unfolded the tissue in her hand and blew her nose as a fresh barrage of tears slipped down her cheeks.

Watching her, a weight settled in Kat's chest. With Rebecca in such obvious distress, Kat couldn't believe she had anything to do with her sister's death. Unfortunately, that conclusion still left her with one unanswered question.

Who had?

CHAPTER TEN

After paying her respects to Rebecca, Kat's spirits were at an all-time low. Having grown up in foster care, she knew better than most people what it was like to not have any relatives, but the thought of having a family—one that could be remembered, anyway—and then losing everyone in it seemed almost unbearable.

At least she had Matty and Tom now, Kat thought as she let herself into her apartment. Although it was the first time in her thirty-two years that she'd ever had pets, she couldn't fathom how she'd lived without them for so long. Even watching them sleep cheered her considerably.

Tom walked over to her and rubbed against her legs as she toed her shoes off. She could hear him purring before she even crouched down to pet him.

“I’m glad to see you too, buddy,” she said. “What did you do while I was away?”

Their reunion was interrupted by a knock on the front door. Frowning, Kat glanced at the clock in the living room, trying to remember if she’d made an appointment she’d forgotten about.

“Kat?” a voice called from outside. “It’s Lucy Callahan.”

Kat tensed. Matty glowered at the door from her spot on the couch, as if to question who dared to interrupt her peace. Tom, on the other hand, crept closer and tried to peek through the crack between the door and the floor. As long as he netted some belly rubs out of the deal, Kat figured he wouldn’t have any issues with a suspected murderer paying them a visit.

Fighting a sigh, Kat stood up and swung the door open. The apartment walls weren’t very thick and she was pretty sure Lucy had already heard her talking to Tom, eliminating any chance she had of fooling her unwanted visitor into thinking she wasn’t home. That was what she got for carrying on conversations with cats, she thought.

Lucy's grinning face came into view. "Hi, neighbor. I was across the way measuring the dimensions of my new apartment when I heard your footsteps in the hallway."

Kat didn't say anything, scrambling for some excuse to retreat back into her unit alone. But what could she say? That she'd only come home to grab something she'd forgotten? She'd already taken off her shoes.

Lucy bounced from foot to foot, craning her neck as she attempted to see into the apartment. "If you're not busy, I thought maybe you could give me some pointers on caring for cats. I need a break anyway."

"Oh, sure." Although she didn't feel like entertaining, Kat held the door open. "Come on in."

Lucy scooted past Tom, who sniffed at her ankles. "Who's this big guy?"

"That's Tom."

Lucy squatted on the floor and ran her hands down Tom's sides. He rolled onto his back and held his paws above his head.

Lucy laughed. "He doesn't waste any time, does he?"

In spite of herself, Kat couldn't help but smile. "He never gets enough."

Lucy peered at Matty, who hadn't budged from her position on the couch. "What about that one? He looks a little more reserved."

"She," Kat corrected. "And yes, Matty is much less of an attention hog."

"Are they related?"

Kat shook her head. "They just have similar colorings."

Lucy leaned closer to Tom and crooned, "Well, I think you're gorgeous, big fellow."

Tom rubbed his face against the carpet as he dragged himself along the floor, basking in the attention.

Matty stood up, tilting her nose in the air as she eyed Lucy and Tom. She jumped off the couch and stalked down the hallway, evidently unable to stand the sight of Tom degrading himself like that any longer.

Kat lowered herself onto the couch. "So, what is it you need help with?"

"Nothing in particular," Lucy replied. "I read a couple articles online about cat care, but I don't trust anything posted on the Internet. Besides, they only touched upon the basics, things like making sure they're fed and cleaning out their litter box. What else do I need to know?"

"Nothing really. Besides that, regular vet visits, and lots of love, they're fairly independent."

Lucy nodded. She didn't look surprised, which made Kat wonder if she'd actually come over to be social.

Tom must have finally gotten his fill of belly rubs. He righted himself and wandered down the hallway. Kat wasn't sure if he was going in search of Matty, his litter box, or a comfortable napping spot. Tom seemed to be under the impression that the queen-sized bed belonged to him.

Lucy relocated to the sofa opposite Kat. "I think I'm going to like having a cat."

"If you're anything like me you will," Kat agreed.

"Did you have to train them to use the box?"

Kat shook her head. "Their mother usually teaches them, assuming they aren't removed from her care too soon. And cats are naturally clean animals. All the ones up for adoption from 4F are already litter-trained."

Lucy relaxed into the couch. "That's good. I was worried about that."

Matty stalked through the room. After disappearing into the kitchen for a moment, she planted herself at the edge of the living room and glared at Kat.

Lucy's mouth crooked. "She's not very friendly, is she?"

"She's very friendly, actually," Kat said, feeling compelled to defend the feline. "She's just not as open with her affection as Tom is. And that look she's giving me means her food bowl is empty, a situation she dislikes immensely."

Lucy stood up, her eyes brightening. "Maybe I could help you feed them. You know, get some practice in."

Kat lifted one shoulder before standing up and heading toward the kitchen. Although she couldn't determine exactly what Lucy thought would be involved with feeding cats other than scooping some kibble into a couple bowls, she didn't want to start off on the wrong foot with her new neighbor—just in case she wasn't a cold-blooded killer.

As soon as Kat opened their food bag, Tom came tearing into the kitchen. He screeched to a stop in front of one of the empty bowls and meowed.

Lucy laughed. "I should have figured that

one likes to eat."

"A hearty appetite is a universal cat quality."

Kat poured some kibble into each of their bowls. Tom tore into the food, wolfing it down as if he hadn't consumed a decent meal in weeks. Matty took a few bites from her portion, then looked over her shoulder at Tom.

"What's she doing?" Lucy asked.

"She's convinced I give him better food," Kat said, her mouth twitching as Matty's tail started to flick back and forth. "Watch."

Sure enough, a second later Matty sauntered over to Tom and proceeded to sit down and stare at him until he became uncomfortable enough to relocate to Matty's food dish. Matty then moved forward and began nibbling from Tom's bowl.

Lucy giggled. "I never would have guessed they were that silly."

Kat laughed along with Lucy but froze mid-chuckle as something occurred to her.

Heidi and Rebecca Smith had ended up in Andrew's and Kat's designated seats at the benefit dinner. The iced teas had been poured before the guests were let into the area. Anyone in attendance could have used the printed place settings to determine where the guests would be sitting—assuming they didn't switch places. It wasn't a stretch to think the poison was already in one of the iced tea glasses before Kat had offered to switch places with the Smiths.

Kat's pulse pounded as her brain tried to wrap itself around the possibility that the poisoned beverage might not have been intended for Heidi at all. Maybe it had been waiting for Kat or Andrew to take that first, fatal sip.

But, for the life of her, Kat couldn't think of anyone who might want to do her harm. She certainly didn't think she had any enemies who hated her enough to kill her.

Andrew, on the other hand, dealt with unsavory characters all the time, she thought, breaking out into a sweat. As a member of the police force, how many criminals had he helped to convict over the years? She didn't know but figured the number was substantial. It wasn't impossible to think one of them might come after him personally.

And if Andrew was the killer's target, she had better warn him before they made another attempt on his life.

Kat whipped toward her guest, her heart feeling as if it might explode out of her chest. "Lucy, would you excuse me? I just remembered

I'm supposed to be somewhere."

"Oh." Lucy's face fell a fraction. "Sure."

Kat briefly considered assuring Lucy that her hasty departure had nothing to do with her, but that would require a delay she didn't want to incur. Instead, she brushed past the startled redhead and raced back into the living room.

Lucy followed more slowly, her forehead furrowed in consternation. "So, maybe we can meet up again later?"

"Okay." Kat snatched her purse off the coffee table, crammed her feet into her shoes, and flew out the front door, almost beating Lucy out of her unit.

Sprinting down the corridor, one question cycled through her mind on autoplay: Who was the intended victim yesterday evening, Heidi Smith, Andrew Milhone, or herself?

CHAPTER ELEVEN

Kat was relieved to find Andrew at the police station. She had been in such a rush to see him she hadn't bothered to call ahead.

He stood up when she barged into his office. "Well, this is a pleasant surprise."

She shut the door and dropped into the visitor seat, winded after running across the parking lot. It was a miracle she hadn't been pulled over for speeding on her way here.

"I need to run something by you," she said breathlessly.

Andrew sat back down and folded his arms on the desk. "I have an update for you too."

"On Heidi's poisoning?" When Andrew nodded, she said, "You go first then."

"That container you recovered from the restroom tested positive for the same type of poison found in Heidi's iced tea."

Although she didn't think it was possible, Kat's heart beat a little faster. "It did?"

"Yep. The lab guys say it was some sort of lye-based substance, similar to what might be found in an industrial cleaning solution."

"Have you been able to link it with anybody?"

Andrew shook his head. "My understanding is that type of product is pretty common."

Kat's heart sank. "So really, the vial doesn't provide you with any leads."

"Nope," Andrew agreed, looking unfazed. "Okay, your turn."

"So, I've been thinking," she began slowly.

"About what happened to Heidi?"

Kat nodded.

Andrew's jaw tensed. "You're not involving yourself in this case, are you?"

"Not really," Kat lied.

He studied her for a long moment, clearly not buying it. But he didn't challenge her.

Kat coughed. "Anyway, I was thinking maybe that cleaning solution wasn't meant to be ingested by Heidi after all."

Andrew picked up a pen and rolled it between the tips of his fingers. "What makes you think that?"

"Because you and I were originally supposed to sit where Heidi and Rebecca ended up."

When Andrew didn't reply right away, she looked at him, her stomach clenching when she envisioned how differently the benefit dinner might have turned out if they hadn't switched places with the Smiths. Instead of sitting here discussing the case with Andrew, she could be sitting at home crying her eyes out while another detective sought justice for his colleague.

"You think the poison was meant for one of us?" Andrew said at last.

"I'm not sure. It's just a thought that had crossed my mind."

"It's certainly an interesting theory." Andrew braced his elbows on the desk. "Okay, run it by me."

Kat tried to find a more comfortable position, but Andrew's tiny office severely limited her range of motion. She finally gave up when her knees banged into the desk for the third time. "Heidi ended up sitting in one of our seats, right?"

"Mine," Andrew confirmed.

Kat had already figured he was the intended victim, but his words still chilled her. She couldn't imagine she would feel any more terrified if she were the person being targeted.

Swallowing hard, Kat said, "That means Heidi likely drank the iced tea originally set out for you. Whoever put that cleaning solution in there might have meant for you to drink it, not Heidi."

"But who would want to kill me?"

"You *are* a police detective," she pointed out. "You don't exactly run across the most law-abiding citizens every day."

He tapped the pen on his desk. "True."

"Maybe somebody you put away once was just released and decided to exact revenge," Kat suggested. "Or it could be somebody you haven't actually convicted yet. Maybe they think the case against them won't be as strong if you're not around to work on it."

Andrew's lips thinned. "Those are rather flimsy reasons for killing me. First of all, I can't see somebody who was recently released from prison risking their newfound freedom by putting out a hit on a cop. Second, CHPD would operate just fine without me. Most of these cases are pretty straightforward. I just put the evidence together to tell a complete story. Almost anybody on the force could do that."

"What about a friend or family member of somebody you put away?" Kat pressed. "Do you think one of them could want you dead?"

Andrew spread his hands. "What would a friend have to gain by crossing over to the wrong side of the law?"

"Revenge for their friend. Don't the friends and families of criminals ever get upset over the trial verdicts?"

"Sure, all the time," Andrew replied. "But killing me isn't going to get their loved one's conviction overturned. The only thing that will do is increase their own chance of going to jail."

Kat snapped her fingers. "Then maybe it was somebody who wanted to be reunited with a person already in jail."

Andrew lifted one eyebrow. "That would have to be one desperate friend."

She slumped into her seat and crossed her arms over her chest. "Well, whoever tried to kill you has to be pretty desperate."

"We're still not sure that poison was meant for me," he reminded her.

He was right, of course, but now that the

idea had popped into her head, she couldn't shake it. "Just promise me you'll be careful until the killer is caught," she pleaded.

"I'm always careful." His expression shifted as he fixed her under his gaze, his penetrating blue eyes sending a flare of heat surging through her insides. "Kat," he said softly, "I'm a trained police officer. Nothing's going to happen to me."

She nodded, praying he wasn't lying.

CHAPTER TWELVE

As Kat left the police station and headed across the parking lot, she was jarred by a series of sharp barks.

She stopped and surveyed the surrounding area but didn't see any dogs. Just as she was about to resume her trek to her car, movement in the distance caught her eye. Squinting, she could make out something jumping in the back seat of a rusted red sedan parked across the street.

Kat veered toward the car, trying to see whether anyone was inside. Although the driver's side window was open halfway, it was much too hot for anyone to leave an animal unattended inside a vehicle. She wouldn't hesitate to storm back into the police station to report this if necessary.

But as she got closer, she saw there was indeed someone in the driver's seat. They were turned around, presumably to calm down the dog—a dog who looked eerily similar to Champ.

"Tasha?" Kat called out, inching across the road after checking for oncoming traffic.

Tasha's head spun toward the window. "Oh, Kat. Hi."

Kat circled around to the passenger side so she wouldn't be standing in the street. "What are you doing here?" she asked, peering through the open window.

Tasha bit her lip. "I was just taking a drive and decided to pull over for a second."

The way Tasha's eyes flitted sideways when she said the words sent a tingling sensation crawling up Kat's back. "You weren't headed anywhere in particular?"

Tasha's gaze drifted to the back seat. "Champ wanted to go out."

Kat glanced at Champ, who had his nose pressed against the back window, his tail wagging. She'd never had a dog, but she suspected they preferred to roam around when they were outside. They didn't typically beg to be loaded up into a car that would then be parked on the side of the road, did they?

She reasoned that Tasha could have been in the process of driving Champ to the park, but that still didn't explain why she was now stopped with no green areas in sight.

Kat stilled as her eyes locked on to a white, plastic bottle on the floor of the back seat. From this distance, she could barely make out the words 'super cleaner.'

Every hair on the back of her neck stood up. She thought back to what Andrew had said about the poison responsible for Heidi's death. The container in Tasha's car certainly looked like the type that might hold an industrial-strength cleaning solution.

"You just went really pale," Tasha said, wrenching Kat back to the present. "Are you feeling okay?"

Kat didn't reply, her mind a whirl as she recalled the extent of Tasha's distress after Heidi had died. Not long after their encounter in the women's room, Kat had found that empty vial almost on top of the garbage can. She could kick herself now for not suspecting that Tasha had thrown it away herself.

"You're not going to faint or anything, are

you?" Tasha said.

"No." Kat tried to muster up a smile but found she couldn't. "I'm fine."

"You certainly don't look fine." Tasha reached across the passenger seat and pushed the door open. "Sit down for a second."

Kat had to strain to hear Tasha's words over the blood rushing through her ears. Her over-worked heart combined with the August heat *had* made her a little woozy. If she didn't sit down there was a very good chance she might pass out.

Besides, if she could keep her composure this might be her chance to coerce Tasha into blurting out something that would confirm her suspicions.

She opened the door the rest of the way and perched on the edge of the seat.

Champ leaned his head over the console and licked her face. Kat nudged him away, the sen-sation of warm dog saliva on her skin doing nothing to help her building nausea.

"Close the door," Tasha said. "I'll turn the AC on until you cool off."

"I'm okay." Kat didn't make any move to pull her dangling legs inside. She wanted to be ready to run if the need arose.

"I said, close the door."

The sharpness of Tasha's voice prompted Kat to turn around. That was when she saw the gun pointed at her.

Time seemed to stop, and every muscle in her body tensed. After an indeterminate number of seconds had passed, she somehow managed to lift her tongue high enough to stammer, "Wh—what are you doing?"

"What does it look like I'm doing? I'm covering my tracks."

"What tracks?"

Tasha rolled her eyes. "Don't play dumb. I saw your expression when you spotted that bottle in the back."

Kat pried her mouth open to deny it, but realized there wasn't much she could say. Even if she hadn't seen what Tasha thought she had, with Tasha holding her at gunpoint there wasn't much chance of walking away now.

"I should have tossed it earlier, but I thought it might come in handy again," Tasha went on. She looked Kat right in the eye. "For when I needed to get rid of your little cop pal."

The air caught in Kat's lungs. "So it *was* Andrew you meant to kill last night."

"Yes. Last week I overheard somebody saying how he was going to attend the 4F dinner. That's when I bought my own ticket and filched that bottle of cleaner from the janitor's closet where I work. I made sure to carry some in my purse in case I found the opportunity to use it." Tasha's face fell. "I never thought I'd end up killing the wrong person."

Kat wrapped her arms around herself as a shiver traveled through her body. The extent of Tasha's premeditation turned her blood cold.

Tasha jabbed the gun into Kat's ribs. "Now get in the car."

Kat reminded herself to breathe as she pulled her legs into the vehicle, despite how each inhale seemed to bring the gun's muzzle that much closer to her skin. Her motions felt rigid and unnatural, as though she were learning to move again after spending months in a coma.

"Good. Now close that door," Tasha ordered.

Kat reached for the door handle, briefly entertaining the wild idea of throwing her body onto the sidewalk. But when her brain kicked into gear a moment later, she realized how pointless such an attempted escape would be. Even if she somehow managed to make it out of the car alive, Tasha would undoubtedly either run her over or shoot her before she could get far enough away.

Kat pulled the door closed, a sickness spreading throughout her insides when she heard the locks engage.

"That's better," Tasha said.

Kat forced her gaze to the driver's side, trying not to panic. She looked out the window, scanning the outside of the police station in search of someone she could signal for help. The parking lot was empty.

Her eyes traveled downward to Tasha's hands, and she wondered if she should make a pass for the gun. Given how it was pressed up against her rib cage, she didn't dare risk it.

As much as she hated the thought, her best option seemed to be to do whatever Tasha wanted until a better opportunity to escape presented itself. Meanwhile, maybe she could keep Tasha talking, giving her more time to think of a way out of this situation.

"I don't understand," Kat began. "What do you have against Andrew?"

Tasha's face darkened. "He put Jake away."

"Your fiancé," Kat filled in.

Tasha nodded. "All he did was drive home

drunk once. Nobody deserves to go to prison for that."

"But he killed two people," Kat reminded her.

Tasha's head reared back as if she'd been slapped. "Not on purpose! And it was snowing. Anybody could have lost control of their car in those conditions."

"The snow was all the more reason why he should have called a cab, or you," Kat argued, a spark of anger penetrating her fear. "Even if the weather did contribute to the accident, his reflexes were compromised."

"I know that," Tasha spat. "And I'm not saying he wasn't in the wrong. But to be convicted of homicide?" She shook her head. "That was completely unnecessary."

"What kind of punishment do you think he deserved instead?"

"Something like community service. Revoke his license or whatever. But not prison. That's going overboard."

Kat didn't say anything. She couldn't help but recall how stricken Rebecca had looked this morning. Kat was pretty sure that from her point of view, Jake couldn't possibly receive a sentence severe enough to fit his crime.

"And your cop pal Andrew is the main reason why Jake's been sent away to rot," Tasha continued, her voice hard. "If he hadn't been so gung ho about building that case, Jake would have gotten a sentence more in line with his crime. Then I wouldn't have been left all alone."

Kat stared at Tasha, the pain etched on her face illuminating her motive with crystal clarity. Tasha wasn't as upset about Jake serving time for vehicular homicide as she was about how she had lost her fiancé as a result. In her mind, *she* was the one being punished for a crime she had no control over.

"What about you?" Kat said, jerking her chin toward the cleaning solution in the back. "What kind of sentence do you think you deserve for deliberately murdering somebody?"

Tasha glared at her. "What I'm doing is making sure justice is served."

"Justice?" Kat scoffed. "You killed an innocent person."

"That was an accident. If Andrew had been sitting where he was supposed to, she never would have died."

Kat's hands curled into fists. If it weren't for the pistol jammed into her side, she would be sorely tempted to reach across the console and strangle the woman seated next to her.

"You know Andrew and Jake used to belong to the same bowling league?" Tasha said. "This was years ago, but my point is that he knew all about Jake's good qualities too. But did he bother to include any of that in his case report?"

"No matter what his relationship with Jake was, he has to present the case as he sees it."

Tasha snorted. "Please. He was the lead detective. He could have convinced the D.A. or the police chief or whoever to go for a lighter sentence. He could have shown Jake some leniency. But did he bother to do any of that? No."

Kat didn't say anything. She knew no matter how she tried to defend Andrew it wouldn't matter. To Tasha, it wasn't a question of whether Jake had deserved his sentence. It was whether she had deserved how that sentence affected her.

Tasha sighed. "We were happy, you know."

"Yeah?"

"Yeah," Tasha said softly. "He was the only guy I've ever loved."

Kat realized the gun was no longer pressed as firmly against her body. If she could distract Tasha with talk of Jake, perhaps she could wrest her weapon away.

"Tell me about him," Kat said, sitting back as if they were just two girlfriends settling in for a chat about relationships.

"He was great. I'd never met anybody like him."

"How'd you meet?" Kat asked, shifting a millimeter closer to the door.

"He rescued me. My car broke down when I was on my way to Seattle. I managed to pull over to the side of the road, but my phone had died, I didn't have a clue what was wrong, and everybody just kept driving by." Tasha smiled. "Then there was Jake, pulling up behind me like a knight on a white horse."

Although Tasha's eyes were on Kat, she didn't seem to be really looking at her. Her face now had a dreamy expression on it, as though she were getting lost in her memories.

"After he fixed up my car, he asked for my number," Tasha said. "He called me later that same day, and that weekend he took me to this fancy restaurant in Wenatchee called . . ."

Kat tuned out as her gaze drifted to the gun. Tasha was no longer gripping it with enough force to cut off the circulation in her fingers. Kat was tempted to make a grab for it, but her palms went sweaty whenever she noticed how close it still was to her ribs. If the gun went off during a struggle the bullet would most likely hit her, even if Tasha didn't have time to aim at anything in particular.

"I mean, he had his faults," Tasha was saying. "Everybody has their faults, right? I wasn't perfect either. But when I was with him everything just seemed easier."

Kat almost jumped out of her skin when Andrew slid into view outside the window.

"Don't move," he said, his voice low and gravelly.

Tasha gasped, her head whipping around. She blanched when her eyes alighted on the service weapon Andrew had aimed squarely at her chest.

Kat choked down a cry of relief. She didn't think she had ever been more thrilled to see anyone in her entire life.

"Wh—what are you doing here?" Tasha stammered.

"Arresting you."

Deciding to take advantage of the situation, Kat fumbled for Tasha's now abandoned gun. She somehow managed to pick it up and toss it through the passenger window in spite of how badly her fingers were trembling.

Andrew didn't even glance in her direction. Kat wasn't sure if he already knew about the gun, or if he was too focused on Tasha to notice what she was doing.

"You need to exit the vehicle," he said. "Slowly."

Tasha's eyes grew wider, but she dutifully reached for the door lock. Her hands were now shaking as violently as Kat's were.

Champ barked and tried to clamber into the front seat. Kat reached behind her and held onto his collar. If Andrew ended up discharging his weapon, she would hate for the Labrador to be injured incidentally.

Andrew took a step backward as Tasha's door creaked open. "Move slowly, and keep your hands where I can see them."

Tasha did as he instructed. The fight seemed to have left her body. Her shoulders were slumped as she unfolded herself from the vehicle.

"Okay, now turn around and put your hands on the roof of the car," Andrew commanded.

Tasha set her palms on the roof. "How did you know it was me?"

"I didn't until I saw you out here holding

Kat hostage." Andrew slipped his firearm into his shoulder holster and exchanged it for a set of handcuffs, which he wasted no time securing around Tasha's wrists.

Confident that she was finally safe, Kat threw the passenger door open and leapt out of the car, gulping in deep breaths of air. Champ scrambled after her, barking as he tried to run to the other side of the vehicle. Kat slipped his leash around her wrist and leaned against the sedan, unsure whether she would be able to restrain him otherwise.

Andrew looked at her over the top of the car. "Backup is on its way."

Kat nodded. Seconds later she saw two uniformed officers charging out of the station. They sprinted through the parking lot and across the street in record time.

Andrew handed over Tasha. "Read her her rights, and I'll meet you all back inside."

"Roger that."

Tasha stole one last mournful glance at Champ as the officers led her away, perhaps already sensing she would never see him again. For that one second, Kat actually felt sorry for her.

Now that the immediate danger had passed,

Kat realized exactly how close she'd come to joining Heidi in the morgue. Her knees buckled, and she collapsed against the car.

"Hey," Andrew said softly, steadying her with a hand under one elbow. "You're okay. You're safe now."

Kat looked up at him, feeling a surge of gratitude. "You showed up just in time."

He grinned. "Lucky for you, I finally broke for lunch. I've been so swamped I didn't have time to eat earlier."

"You have no idea how glad I am right now for your heavy workload."

"You can thank Chief for that. I'm taking back everything I said yesterday about him not being a slave driver."

Kat laughed. Although she still felt weak, some of her strength was returning.

"Did you catch anything Tasha said in the car?" she asked.

"Just enough to get the gist of things." Andrew looked around before his eyes landed on hers again. "I'll fill in the blanks when I take your statement. Afterward, why don't you come to Jessie's with me? I'll buy you a milkshake."

She glanced at Champ, who hadn't stopped whimpering since Tasha had disappeared into the police station. He kept pacing back and forth, his eyes fixed on the station entrance.

Kat's heart went out to the dog. "I'd love to, but I need to attend to Champ," she told Andrew. "He's pretty agitated."

"What are you going to do with him?"

"I'll call Imogene so we can place him with a foster home." She frowned. "Assuming Tasha won't be able to care for him anymore, he's now officially homeless again."

"If you'd like, I'll give you both a ride to Imogene's." Andrew regarded her, his head slanted in concern. "You don't look like you're in any shape to be driving at the moment."

She couldn't argue with him there. With the adrenaline rush rapidly wearing off, her knees felt as if they were made of jelly.

"Then I'll take your statement and buy you that milkshake." His eyes twinkled. "Maybe I'll even convince Jessie to add a little shot of something to the mix."

She smiled, holding onto his arm as she took a step forward. "How can I refuse an offer like that?"

CHAPTER THIRTEEN

Kat was enjoying a quiet evening at home that night when her cell phone rang. She was all set to ignore it until she glimpsed Andrew's name on the caller ID.

"Hi," she answered, muting the television.

"Hi, yourself," Andrew replied. "Are you busy?"

"Right now?" Kat glanced at Matty and Tom curled up next to her on the sofa. "Not really."

"I'd like to come over and personally thank you for solving my case," he said. "If it weren't for you, who knows what Tasha might have tried when I left the station this afternoon."

His statement sent a shiver down Kat's spine. She dreaded to think of what Tasha had planned for Andrew when she'd camped out in front of his place of employment with a gun in the front seat and a bottle of toxic cleaner in the back.

"I'm only a couple blocks from your apartment," Andrew continued. "Mind if I stop by?"

"No." Kat reflexively patted her hair into place. "Come on over."

They disconnected, and she threw her phone onto the coffee table before flying into the bathroom. She was able to give herself a two-minute makeup refresher before Andrew rang from downstairs and she buzzed him in.

Her stomach fluttered as she waited for him to make it up to her unit. She itched to open the door so there would be no delays when he did arrive, but thought that might make her seem too anxious.

As Kat strained to detect any sounds from the hallway, Matty watched her with one eye open, clearly wondering if her human had gone bonkers. Tom had evidently decided her restless energy was good for something and ambled over for some attention.

Kat only managed one scratch between Tom's ears before a knock on the door made her jump two feet into the air. She spun around and swung the door open.

Andrew smiled at her as he stepped inside. “Hi.”

“Hey.” She shut the door behind him.

“Hi, big guy,” Andrew said, reaching down to rub Tom, who rolled onto the floor to expose his belly.

“Can I get you something to drink?” Kat offered.

“Nah, I just wanted to stop by for a minute since I was in the neighborhood.”

“Oh.” Kat tried to push her disappointment aside.

Andrew looked up at her, a hank of hair falling onto his forehead. “I’ve been thinking about this whole poisoning thing and how close I came to being in Heidi’s seat.”

Kat wrapped her arms around herself, trying not to shudder from the reminder.

“It’s really made me reflect on how short life can be,” Andrew said, turning his attention back to Tom.

Kat swallowed, remembering Lucy Callahan’s almost identical words from that morning. Now, she felt a little bad for ever suspecting her new neighbor of killing another woman.

Andrew gave Tom one last pat before standing up and facing Kat. "Anyway, it's gotten me thinking that we really shouldn't waste our time here on earth."

Kat nodded. Her insides twisted into a knot whenever she thought of how close she'd come to losing Andrew so soon after finding him again.

"You know, I was really looking forward to the benefit dinner," he said.

"I was too," Kat admitted.

Andrew's gaze drifted to Matty before he refocused on Kat. "Since that meal didn't turn out quite the way we'd planned, maybe you'd let me take you out some other time."

Kat smiled. "I'd like that."

"Kind of like a date," Andrew went on, lacing his fingers together. "Except with food I've heard of." His mouth quirked for a second before the expression faded away.

He's nervous, Kat realized with a jolt. The observation cheered her.

"I'd like that," she said again, somewhat more confidently now that she knew her feelings weren't entirely one-sided.

Andrew's posture relaxed. "Okay. Good. So, does Saturday work for you?"

Kat glanced around. The television was

playing some program she couldn't even remember turning on. Her gaze alighted on Matty, who stared at her as if silently communicating that Kat would be an idiot not to accept.

Kat turned back around to face Andrew. "We could go now if you're free. I'm not doing anything."

His eyes sparkled. "Okay."

Kat flicked the TV off and grabbed her purse and phone off of the coffee table. She wished she had more time to prepare for an actual date but didn't want to keep Andrew waiting while she vacillated between outfits. Besides, knowing he was sitting in the next room would make her too nervous to master anything as complicated as a button or a zipper.

She stuffed her phone into her purse and hooked the strap over her shoulder. "I'm ready."

Andrew frowned. "You don't have any shoes on."

"Oh, fiddlesticks." Kat grabbed her sneakers off the floor and shoved them on her feet.

Andrew laughed. "I see you're still using that expression."

She stuck her tongue out at him as she tied her shoelaces. "You should be used to it by now."

She had just joined Andrew by the front door when his fingers encircled her arm. The gesture caught her off guard, and she almost stumbled face-first into the wall.

"There's just one thing I have to do before we go," he whispered, leaning closer.

He kissed her, the act surprising her so much it knocked the wind out of her lungs. When she finally registered what was happening, she threaded her fingers through his hair and pulled him closer, relaxing into him as she returned the kiss. Every bone in her body felt as if it were melting.

After what struck her as too short a moment, Andrew pulled back. His eyes were soft, and a smile played on his lips. "Sorry, I wasn't planning that."

She took a deep breath, but the extra oxygen did nothing to slow her pounding heart. Her whole body felt close to combusting. "It's okay."

"Seize the moment and all that," he said, gripping the doorknob.

Kat glanced over her shoulder as she adjusted her hold on her purse. Tom had rejoined Matty on the couch. Both cats were watching her with huge eyes, looking shell-shocked by what they'd just witnessed.

Kat shrugged at them, abnormally happy in spite of everything that had happened in the past thirty-six hours.

"So where do you want to eat?" Andrew asked.

"How about at Jessie's?" she suggested. "I'm in the mood for an extra large milkshake."

He smiled and held the door open for her. "Sounds good. You can never have too many milkshakes."

As she stepped forward, she couldn't help but think that maybe life was really just a series of accidents and tragic events that somehow worked out if you were one of the lucky ones who survived. How else would she have ended up with Matty and Tom in her life?

And now, it looked like, Kat thought with a smile, Andrew Milhone.

NOTE FROM THE AUTHOR

Thank you for visiting Cherry Hills, home of Kat and Matty! If you enjoyed their story, please consider leaving a book review on your favorite retailer and/or review site.

Keep reading for an excerpt from Book Four of the Cozy Cat Caper Mystery series, *Vanished in Cherry Hills*. Thank you!

VANISHED *in* CHERRY HILLS

Is it possible to track down someone who doesn't want to be found?

Kat Harper spent most of her childhood in foster care, being raised by strangers while the woman who gave her life quietly slipped into the shadows. Now in her thirties, Kat longs to locate the mother she barely remembers.

Little does she know, so do the police.

It turns out, Kat's mother is suspected of a crime that's gone unsolved for thirty years. And if Kat is successful in her quest, her mother might reenter her life only to spend her remaining years behind bars.

Torn between her greatest wish and her biggest fear, Kat's not sure what to do. Living in darkness for another thirty years isn't an option, but will her need for answers end up forever alienating the one person she yearns to connect with most?

* * *

Please check your favorite online retailer for availability.

Excerpt From

VANISHED *in* CHERRY HILLS

PAIGE SLEUTH

"I want to find my mother," Katherine Harper said.

Andrew Milhone's hand stilled, the mashed potatoes he had been about to shovel into his mouth freezing in front of him.

Kat looked at a couple sitting on the other side of the restaurant to help steady herself. Her heart had revved up the moment she'd mentioned her mother, and she felt a little dizzy.

When Andrew still hadn't spoken after a long moment had passed, she turned back to him. "Did you hear me? I want to find my mother."

"I heard you."

She folded her hands in her lap. "I have to admit, I thought you'd be more surprised about me wanting to look for her after all these years."

He set down his fork. "I am surprised. I mean, I was expecting this, but I didn't expect you to just blurt it out like that on our first date."

She frowned. "It's our second date."

Andrew regarded her as if she'd announced she wanted to dance a jig on top of their table. "It's our first date. I would recall if we'd been out before."

She gaped at him. "We went to Jessie's Diner last week."

He waved his hand. "Drinking a couple milkshakes at Jessie's doesn't count."

She looked around to make sure the waitress wasn't anywhere nearby before hunching closer and whispering, "You kissed me before we left my apartment."

He grinned, his adorable dimples making an appearance. "I know. It was a pretty good kiss too."

Kat couldn't prevent the flush that crept up her cheeks. It *was* a good kiss. She couldn't argue with him there.

"But one kiss doesn't turn a visit to Jessie's into a proper date," Andrew continued.

Kat lifted up her wineglass and took a sip, considering his point. "No, but you footing the bill does. If it weren't a date, we would have gone dutch."

"You used your employee discount," he countered.

"So?" He opened his mouth but she held up her hand before he could say anything. "And we're getting off topic."

He pushed a hank of sandy hair off his forehead. "Right. You want to find your mother."

She nodded, the lighthearted intermission fading as rapidly as it had appeared. "I've been thinking about what you said last week, about how life is short and we only have so much time."

His eyes softened. "I remember."

She set her wineglass down, unable to hold it steady now that her hand had started shaking. "If I don't find her now, I'm afraid I'll never know what happened to make her abandon me. What if she dies before I get the chance to talk to her?"

Andrew covered one of her hands with his. "Have you considered that she might not be alive?"

Kat blanched. Although she'd given a fleeting thought to the idea, it had been too unpleasant to dwell on for very long.

"You can't rule out the possibility," Andrew

said softly. "Given her history."

Kat swallowed. "As a drug addict, you mean."

Andrew nodded.

She straightened. "Well, alive or not, I feel compelled to look for her. I have so many unanswered questions about my past, questions only she can answer. Growing up in foster care, it's like I always felt there was this huge hole in my life. She's the only one who can even come close to filling it. I don't want to spend forever always wondering if I should have looked for her or regretting that I never made an effort to reach out." She knew she was rambling and cut herself off with a deep breath.

"I don't want to talk you out of it. I just want you to be prepared for whatever we find."

She nodded, knowing he wasn't trying to be negative. As a police detective, she figured he was simply programmed to expect the worst.

Andrew squeezed her hand. "And I definitely want to help."

Although Kat knew he would, hearing his words lifted a huge weight from her shoulders. Still, she had no clue how to go about looking for a woman she didn't remember and hadn't seen in three decades.

"So, where do we start?" she asked, hoping

Andrew would know.

"We'll see what information we can dig up and go from there."

Kat nodded, her mind churning. "I could search around on the Internet."

"That would be wise. I know you're a computer whiz."

She rolled her eyes. "I'm not a whiz. I'm just more comfortable with them than you are."

He grinned. "Right."

Kat picked up her fork and played with it, needing to do something with her hands. "Do you think she's still in Washington State?"

"Kat." Andrew looked into her eyes. "I'd just be speculating if I said anything."

She knew he was right, but her brain wouldn't rest. Despite spending most of her thirty-two years trying to forget about the woman who had given her life, now that she'd made the decision to track her down she felt an urgency that hadn't been there before.

Kat shifted in her seat, anxious to get moving. "When do you want to begin?"

Andrew motioned the waitress over. "As soon as I pay the bill."

* * *

Please check your favorite online retailer for availability.

ABOUT THE AUTHOR

Paige Sleuth is a pseudonym for mystery author Marla Bradeen. She plots murder during the day and fights for mattress space with her two rescue cats at night. When not attending to her cats' demands, she writes. Find her at: http://www.marlabradeen.com